THE BIG GOLDEN BOOK OF
DINOSAURS

By Mary Elting

Illustrated by Christopher Santoro

A GOLDEN BOOK • NEW YORK

Western Publishing Company, Inc., Racine, Wisconsin 53404

Writing a book about dinosaurs is almost as exciting as digging up their bones. Not quite. But it does mean reading innumerable books and articles, new and old, and talking with people who are intent on finding out what really went on all those millions of years ago. For hours with books and diggers I am grateful, and I owe special thanks to Dr. Robert Bakker, who was kind enough to read my manuscript and make valuable suggestions.

—Mary Elting

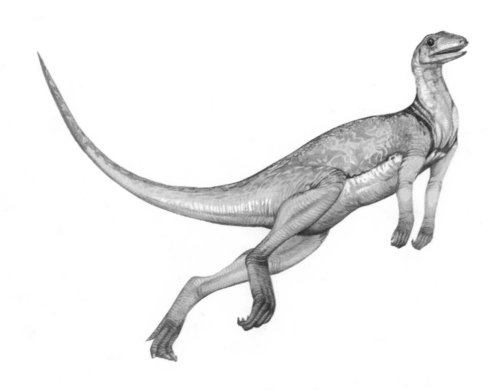

To Natalie—C.S.

To the girls and boys
of McElwain Elementary School in Denver
and to Ruth Sawdo, whose fourth grade students
led the spirited and successful lobby
to make Stegosaurus Colorado's
official state fossil. —M.E.

Look Out, Little Dinosaur!

Just in time, this baby dinosaur's mother saw that it was in danger. She quickly shooed it back to safety.

The huge meat-eater started to follow them. Then it stopped. It saw a whole herd of angry mothers stamping and snorting and forming a circle around all their babies. The fierce giant knew what those sharp horns could do if they rammed into it. That day it went away hungry.

The name of the big meat-eater is Gorgosaurus. The mothers and babies belonged to a family we call styracosaurs.

Baby dinosaurs weren't always so lucky. Sometimes they did not escape. How do we know? Scientists have found the bones of a little dinosaur along with the large tooth of a meat-eater. The tooth probably broke off while the meat-eater was biting.

Dinosaur bones are different from the bones of animals that died just a little while ago. They have been buried in the ground for millions of years and are now as hard as rocks. These rocklike bones are called fossils.

The styracosaurs and Gorgosaurus lived almost 70 million years ago. That was long before there were any people in the world. Still, they were not the first dinosaurs on Earth. Millions of years before the little styracosaur had its narrow escape, many very different dinosaurs had already lived and died. Their bones, too, became fossils.

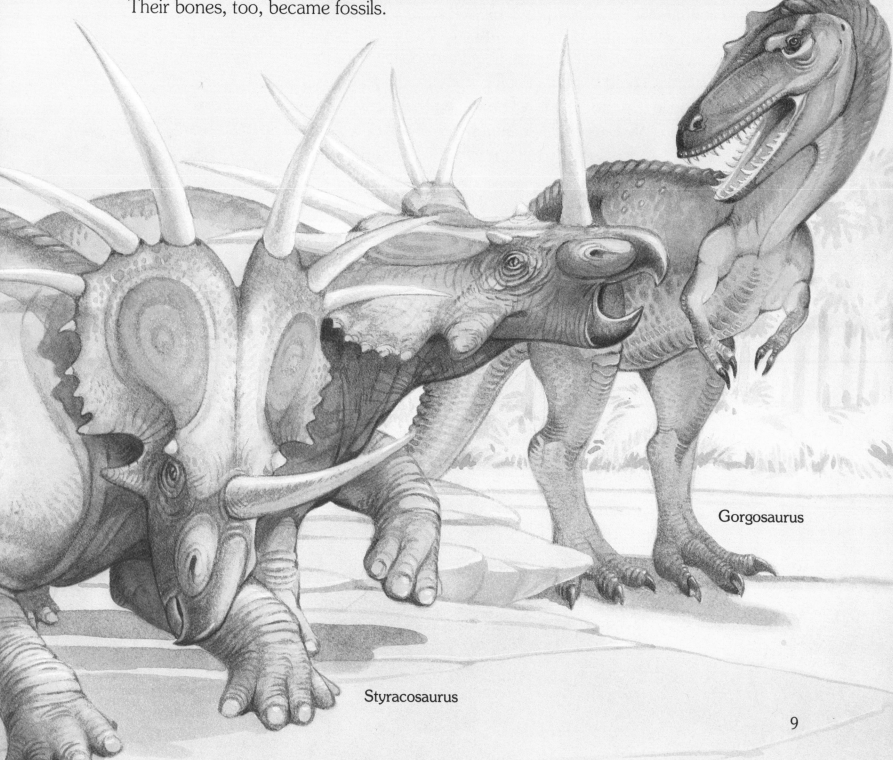

Gorgosaurus

Styracosaurus

The First Dinosaurs

For years people studied truckloads of fossil bones, looking for an answer to this question: What creature was the first dinosaur? The answer began to take shape when a scientist dug up the bones of tiny Lagosuchus, which was only about the size of a chicken.

At first nobody was sure what kind of animal Lagosuchus really was. Its name means "rabbit-crocodile," because it was a little bit like both those animals.

Lagosuchus had long legs and feet that would have helped it leap like a rabbit. And it had a strong tail, like a crocodile's. But its neck was different. Lagosuchus could bend its neck into a curve. That is something no rabbit or crocodile can do. But it is something that early dinosaurs *could* do. Lagosuchus also seemed like a member of the dinosaur family in so many other ways that scientists think it was the very first one.

Lagosuchus

Coelophysis

Lagosuchus lived about 225 million years ago. Scientists know it was a meat-eater because it had teeth like sharp little daggers that slashed and tore apart the smaller creatures it caught and ate.

Other dagger-toothed, meat-eating dinosaurs appeared after a while. One of the early ones was Coelophysis, which had hollow bones. That meant its body was very light, so it could run very fast to catch its prey.

Sometimes these feisty hunters stayed in a group. Together they would chase and gobble up bigger animals. How do we know Coelophysis gathered in herds? A scientist once found the fossil skeletons of dozens of them in one place. Perhaps they were all hunting together when they died in an accident such as a landslide.

11

12

A New Shape

In the beginning, dinosaurs were not very large. When Coelophysis stood on its hind feet, it was only about as high as a six-foot-tall man. The first really big dinosaur that we know about is Plateosaurus. It was twice as tall as Coelophysis and much heavier.

Plateosaurus had sharp teeth, but they were not as knifelike as the teeth of meat-eating Coelophysis. Most scientists believe Plateosaurus was a plant-eater that fed on green leaves.

Unlike the slim meat-eaters, Plateosaurus had a huge belly. There is a good reason for the difference. Meat digests quickly, and Coelophysis' small stomach could soon take care of a large dinner. But tough green leaves are hard to digest. An animal as big as Plateosaurus needed a stomach with plenty of space where plant food could churn and slosh around for hours.

Plateosaurus had very strange fingers on its front paws. It could use the large claws on its thumbs to pull down branches from tall trees when it was standing on its hind feet. After it finished eating, Plateosaurus would fold the ends of its fingers backward. This turned the claws up out of the way, so Plateosaurus could walk comfortably on all four feet.

But Plateosaurus did not stand on its hind feet just to get food. Like many other plant-eaters, it would rise up and use its claws to beat off a meat-eater's attack.

Lesothosaurus

The Munchers

Some early plant-eating dinosaurs looked very much like meat-eaters. They were small, with strong hind legs, and could run as fast as the meat-eaters. But their teeth were not so much like steak knives.

Plant-eating Lesothosaurus had smooth, pointed front teeth. It used them to nip off green leaves. The teeth in the sides of its jaws looked something like arrowheads. Lesothosaurus used them to munch and slice up the leaves before it swallowed them.

14

Lesothosaurus lived in a part of the world that became a desert for several months each year. When the plants dried up and died, what did Lesothosaurus eat? Some scientists say it just curled up in a cave and went to sleep until rains brought the plants to life again. Why do they think so? One clue is Lesothosaurus' teeth. Sometimes the teeth that scientists find are scratched and worn down. This is probably from cutting tough leaves. But other Lesothosaurus teeth that have been discovered look smooth and unused. It is possible that the worn teeth dropped out and new ones grew in while Lesothosaurus was asleep and not eating.

Another early plant-eater, Heterodontosaurus, also had puzzling teeth—three different kinds. Sharp front teeth nipped off leaves. Ridged back teeth munched and crushed the food. But in between were big fangs. Usually it was the meat-eaters who had fangs. Perhaps Heterodontosaurus used its fangs for fighting back when attacked.

Heterodontosaurus

Dimorphodon

Icarosaurus

16

Other Early Creatures

The early dinosaurs shared Earth with many other animals. Little creatures called pterosaurs soared over water on leathery wings, swooping down to snatch fish. Although they could fly, they were not birds. In those days no birds lived anywhere on Earth. The pterosaur Dimorphodon could fly very well, but it also had strong legs. It could run along the beach to catch insects or small lizardlike creatures.

A strange animal named Tanystropheus lived on the beach. It probably stretched out its long neck like a fishing pole and nabbed anything that swam by.

Near the shore, Nothosaurus paddled around, hunting for fish. Farther out, Ichthyosaurus, with its huge eyes, could find food even in deep, dim water.

Ichthyosaurus' fossil bones were discovered not by scientists but by an eleven-year-old girl named Mary Anning. And two high-school boys were the first to discover Icarosaurus, a tiny early creature that looked like a hang glider. Its ribs, covered with a web of skin, stuck out from its sides like wings, but it could not fly. It glided from tree to tree, hunting for insects. So did Longisquama, which could fold its wings up over its back.

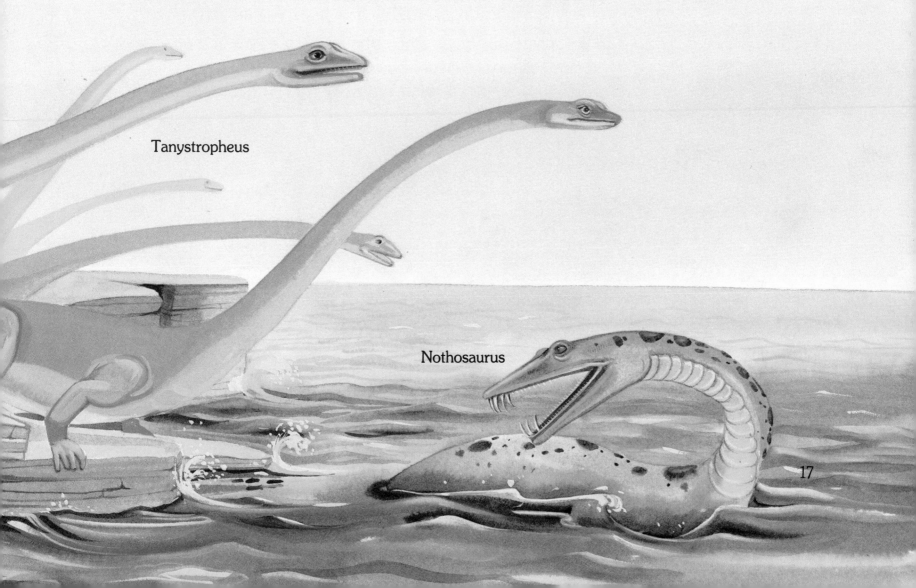

Tanystropheus

Nothosaurus

17

Here Come the Giants

After millions of years, the early dinosaurs and many other early animals disappeared. No one knows why. But in the meantime, entirely different kinds of dinosaurs made their appearance on Earth.

Some of the new plant-eating dinosaurs were huge and heavy and had long necks. Instead of holding their front paws off the ground when they walked, they went about on all fours. They belonged to a family called sauropods. The earliest one we know about was Barapasaurus. Its bones were found in India.

Barapasaurus weighed as much as three elephants, and its neck was so long that it could eat the tops of trees twenty feet tall. That means Barapasaurus was more than three times as tall as a grown man.

Why did the sauropods grow so big? This probably happened because they had plenty of food. There were many great forests in the world, and dinosaurs could wander from one to another, feeding for hours and hours every day on evergreen leaves and the tops of tall fern trees. The more they ate, the bigger they grew. Perhaps during their whole lives they never stopped growing, and they may have lived a hundred years or more.

Big new meat-eaters lived at the same time as Barapasaurus. Scientists found out about one of them, Dilophosaurus, when a Navaho Indian discovered its bones on the Navaho reservation in Arizona.

Dilophosaurus

Barapasaurus

19

Camarasaurus

Allosaurus

A House Made of Bones

Scientists use dinosaur bones to figure out what those ancient creatures looked like and how they lived. Jaw bones help to tell how a dinosaur chewed and what it ate. Large rough places on bones show where strong muscles were attached. But the strangest of all uses for dinosaur bones surprised some fossil hunters in Wyoming. One day they found a small building that looked rather like a log cabin. A sheepherder had built it for himself—but not from logs. He had made it from huge dinosaur bones!

Just beyond Bone Cabin the fossil hunters discovered more enormous bones. Dinosaurs had lived and died there millions of years before. One of them was the giant Camarasaurus.

Camarasaurus

Camarasaurus had an unusual skull. Far up on its face were two very large holes separated by a ridge of bone. Very large nostrils must have filled the holes when Camarasaurus was alive. What could have been the use of such a big nose? Some scientists think it may have been shaped something like an elephant's trunk, but much shorter. Perhaps by blowing through its trunk, Camarasaurus could snort and toot the way elk and some other animals do today.

Camarasaurus had to watch out for the fierce meat-eater Allosaurus, which could move quickly on its strong-muscled hind legs. Allosaurus was big and powerful enough to attack even a large plant-eater, and its teeth cut like great steak knives.

Diplodocus

Fossil collectors discovered the skeleton of another dinosaur not far from Bone Cabin. This one, called Diplodocus, was even longer and taller than Camarasaurus. At first everyone thought that such an enormous creature would have gotten too tired walking around on dry land. They said it must have spent most of its life in lakes or swampy places where water would help to support its heavy body. Such an animal, they thought, must have eaten mushy water plants.

Diplodocus, like Camarasaurus, had a hole for nostrils at the top of its head. This made most people think it was a snorkeler. When it stood in deep water, they said, its long neck would keep the nostrils out in the air so Diplodocus could breathe.

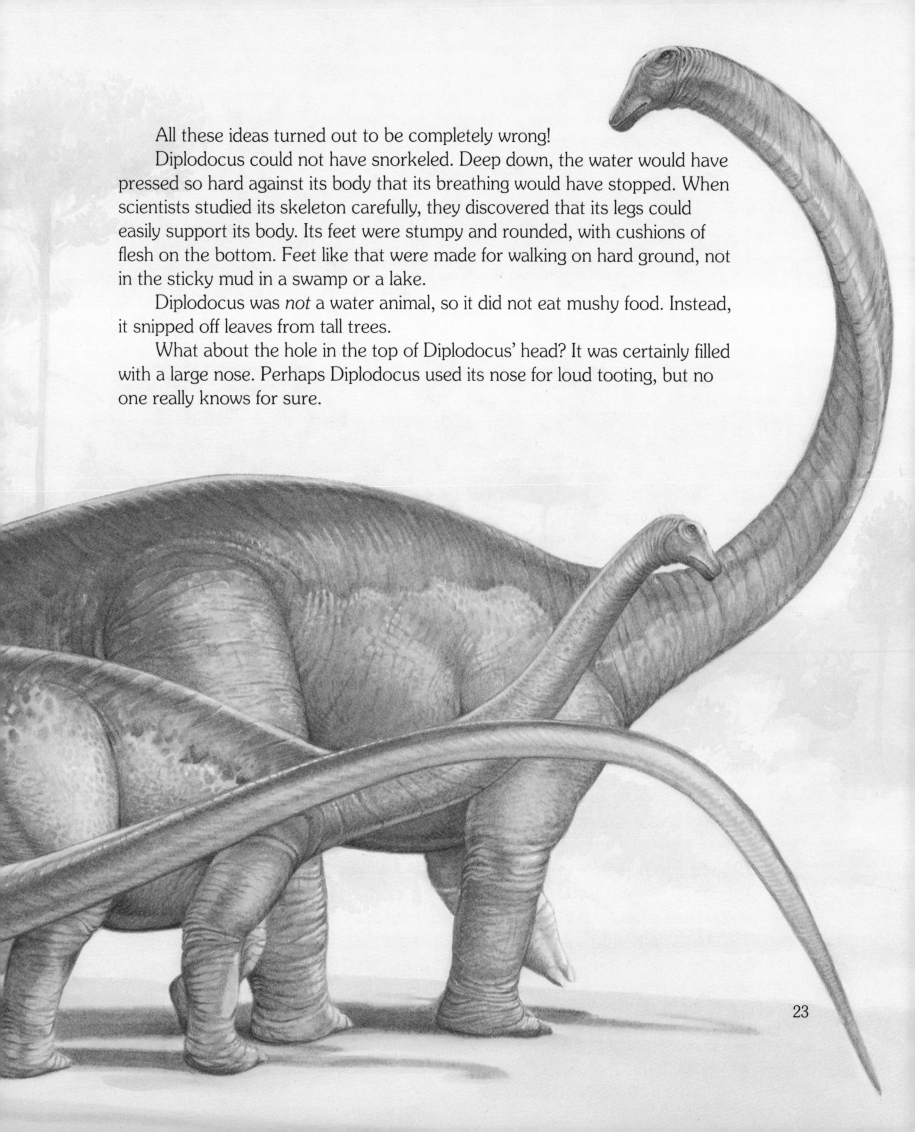

All these ideas turned out to be completely wrong!

Diplodocus could not have snorkeled. Deep down, the water would have pressed so hard against its body that its breathing would have stopped. When scientists studied its skeleton carefully, they discovered that its legs could easily support its body. Its feet were stumpy and rounded, with cushions of flesh on the bottom. Feet like that were made for walking on hard ground, not in the sticky mud in a swamp or a lake.

Diplodocus was *not* a water animal, so it did not eat mushy food. Instead, it snipped off leaves from tall trees.

What about the hole in the top of Diplodocus' head? It was certainly filled with a large nose. Perhaps Diplodocus used its nose for loud tooting, but no one really knows for sure.

Brontosaurus

Footprints Tell the Story

A group of dinosaurs related to Diplodocus once came to drink at the edge of a lake in Colorado. They were much heavier than Diplodocus. In fact, they were so heavy that scientists imagined their huge feet made a great noise when they walked. That is why they were given the name Brontosaurus, which means "thunder lizard." Sometimes they are called Apatosaurus.

As these brontosaurs marched along the damp lakeshore, they left deep, rounded holes in the mud. Later the mud dried out and finally turned to stone, with the footprints still showing. Now, millions of years later, when scientists find these fossil tracks, they can tell what animal made them.

Camptosaurus

While the brontosaurs were drinking, a different kind of dinosaur joined them. These were smaller plant-eaters called camptosaurs. A whole herd of them left their three-toed footprints in the mud.

At the same time, first one Allosaurus and then another came up and lurked nearby. These meat-eaters watched and waited for a young Camptosaurus to leave its mother. But not one strayed from the herd, and the meat-eaters had no dinner at this place.

How do we know? The plant-eaters' tracks were all made by animals who felt safe. If they were alarmed or attacked, their footprints would show that they were scuffling or running back and forth. Instead, they all just walked slowly and quietly away.

25

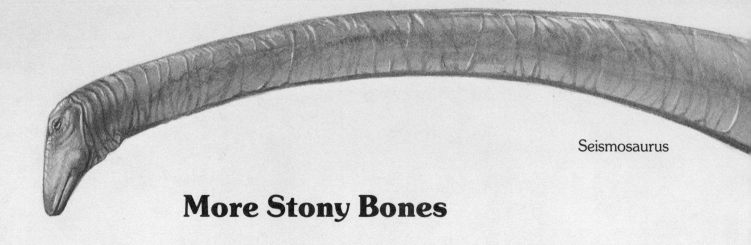
Seismosaurus

More Stony Bones

One day two men were hiking up a hill in New Mexico. At the top of the ridge, one of them looked down at some rocks and yelled, "Hey, what's this?"

The rocks had an unusual shape. They looked like parts of the backbone or the tail of a very large animal, and that is exactly what they were—stony fossil bones.

The two men persuaded a scientist to take a look at their discovery. As they dug earth away from the bones they got more and more excited. They found parts of leg bones, too. This was a whopping big cousin of Diplodocus. When it put down one heavy foot after another, the ground must have trembled. The scientist nicknamed it "Seismosaurus," which means that it made the earth quake.

Like Diplodocus, this earth-shaker had an extremely long tail. Perhaps both animals used the tail like a whip to drive off meat-eaters that threatened them.

Another cousin of Diplodocus was Mamenchisaurus, the bones of which were found in China. Mamenchisaurus had the longest dinosaur neck ever discovered. Its neck was almost as long as the rest of its body plus the tail.

Mamenchisaurus

The Biggest of the Big

Imagine eight acrobats standing on each other's shoulders, one above the other. The top acrobat's nose would be just about level with the nose of a certain dinosaur skeleton. The dinosaur is called Brachiosaurus.

A live brachiosaur was more than 40 feet tall, and it weighed about 45 tons. That is as much as 20 big station wagons would weigh, piled up together. A lot of the dinosaur's weight, of course, was flesh, not bones. Brachiosaurus had to carry around tons of skin and muscle—plus all the gallons of food in its stomach. So it had to have a strong skeleton. Some of its bones were thick and solid. But its neck bones and backbones and even its ribs were built with hollow places in them. This made them light but strong. Birds also have hollow places in their bones, and the hollows contain tubes filled with air. Perhaps Brachiosaurus also had some airy bones.

For many years everyone thought the 40-foot Brachiosaurus was the biggest animal that ever lived on land. Then one day a scientist dug an amazing fossil shoulder bone out of the ground in Colorado. It was like a Brachiosaurus shoulder bone, but it was larger. The dinosaur it belonged to was taller than Brachiosaurus, too. It was so enormous that the scientist named it Ultrasaurus, but in fact, it was just a super big brachiosaur.

Huge and Mean

The scientist who dug up Ultrasaurus had two friends who often hiked around in the mountains, hoping to find a place for a uranium mine. Instead, they discovered the bones of a new giant meat-eater with big wicked claws. The scientist named it Torvosaurus. Torvo means "cruel" or "mean."

No matter how mean Torvosaurus was, it probably didn't try to attack the plant-eater Stegosaurus. Stegosaurus may have looked like an awkward, slow animal, but it was not. It had tremendous muscles in its hind legs and tail. It could whirl around, swing its tail, and badly wound any meat-eater that came near it.

Scientists love to talk about dinosaurs, and often they disagree. For instance, they have different ideas about the big leaf-shaped plates of bone on Stegosaurus' back. Inside the plates are many hollow tubes that may have held blood vessels. Some scientists think that the blood worked like water in the radiator of a car to cool off Stegosaurus on hot days.

Torvosaurus

Other scientists think the plates flapped up and down to protect Stegosaurus' back from a meat-eater's bite. Still others say the tall bones were a kind of ornament that may have attracted a mate.

For a long time almost everyone agreed that Stegosaurus' bony plates stood in two rows along its back. Then an artist who made dinosaur models for a museum studied Stegosaurus carefully and decided that the plates stood in a single row. Scientists are still discussing that idea.

Stegosaurus

The Mystery of the Feathers

Scientists do agree that huge Torvosaurus had a very tiny relative called Compsognathus. But no one even knew about Compsognathus until one day when a man broke apart two layers of a certain smooth rock. The layers opened like the pages of a book, and between them was the almost perfect little fossil skeleton of Compsognathus.

An even more exciting fossil skeleton lay hidden in that same kind of rock. At first the men who found it thought it was just another little Compsognathus. Then they looked again. The small animal had feathers and wings! Scientists named it Archaeopteryx, which means "ancient wing." But was it a feathered dinosaur—or the first bird?

Compsognathus

Archaeopteryx

If Archaeopteryx was a bird, it must have been a warm-blooded animal. That means its body produced its own heat, and its feathers held in the warmth.

But suppose Archaeopteryx was a dinosaur. When Archaeopteryx was discovered, almost everyone thought that dinosaurs were cold-blooded animals like snakes and lizards. That means they depended on the sun to keep warm. If Archaeopteryx was a cold-blooded dinosaur, then why did it need feathers? And if it was a warm-blooded dinosaur, does that mean *all* dinosaurs were really warm-blooded? Some scientists say yes. Some say no. And some think that certain kinds of dinosaurs could make their own body heat, while other kinds had to rely on the sun. Archaeopteryx is still a mystery.

33

The Terrible Hunters

A lively little meat-eating dinosaur called Deinonychus was so strong and speedy that some scientists think it must have been warm-blooded. Some cold-blooded animals, such as lizards, can scoot along very fast for a short while. Then they have to rest. But Deinonychus had big leg muscles and could easily chase after its dinner without getting tired.

Deinonychus had big shoulder muscles, too. Its arms could reach out and catch another animal in a tight grip. Then it would pounce and kick with its hind feet and rip with the great claws on its middle toes. That is why its name means "terrible claw."

Sometimes a herd of Deinonychuses hunted together. Eight of them once chased and killed a large plant-eater called Tenontosaurus. But while they were eating, a mysterious accident happened. Something buried the eight hunters and Tenontosaurus all at the same time. Scientists know this because all of their fossil bones were found together.

Iguanodon

It would have taken a whole herd of Deinonychuses to kill a grown-up Iguanodon. And even then the little meat-eaters would surely have been stabbed by the sharp spikes on Iguanodon's thumbs.

Bones from dozens of Iguanodon skeletons have been dug up and put together in museums. Some of the skeletons are arranged to make this big plant-eater look as if it walked on its hind feet, with its heavy tail drooping. But now scientists have a different idea. When they studied Iguanodon, they paid special attention to its tail. The tail was very stiff, and Iguanodon held it almost straight out as it marched along with all four feet on the ground.

Some scientists think that baby Iguanodons began walking on their hind legs but then traveled on all fours after they grew up.

If Iguanodon wanted to strike at a meat-eater like Deinonychus, it would rise up and use the spikes on its front paws. It also used its front paws to gather food. But instead of bending its thumb the way we do to hold something, it curved its pinky finger across its palm to grasp a branch or a bunch of leaves.

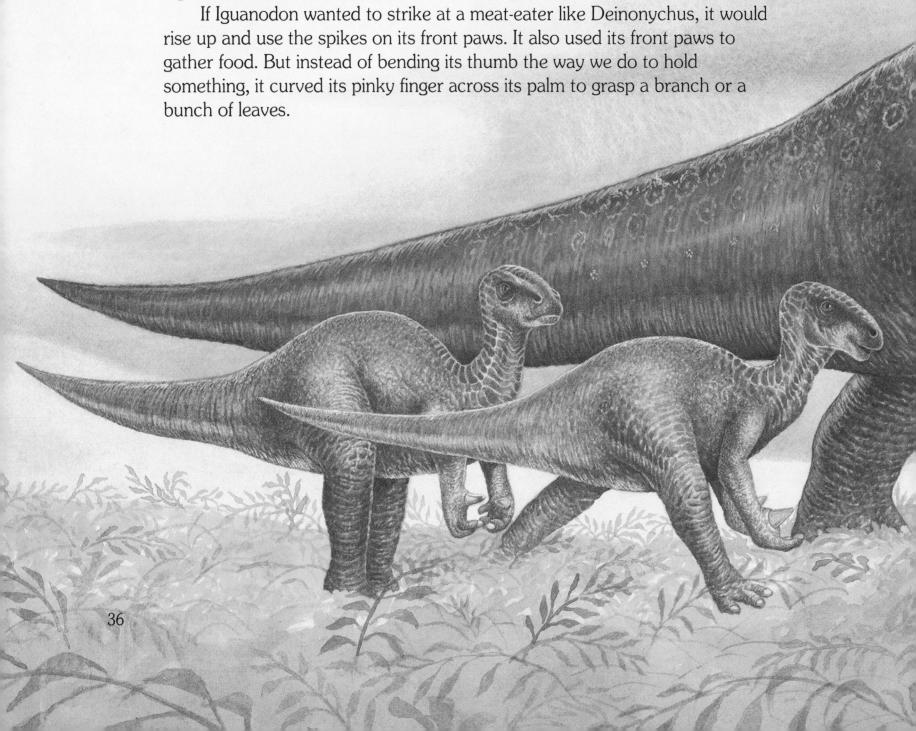

Spinosaurus

Strange Bones and Claws

Iguanodon had a cousin called Ouranosaurus. The two were alike in many ways, except for the long spines that stuck straight up from Ouranosaurus' backbone. The spines were covered with a web of skin and looked like a sail.

Ouranosaurus fed on low plants in the desertlike place where it lived, and it had to worry that the meat-eater Spinosaurus might come prancing after it at any moment. The strange thing is that Spinosaurus, too, had a "sail" on its back—an enormous one, eight feet high. What use did these dinosaurs have for their "sails"? Did they work like radiators on hot days? No one knows.

Ouranosaurus

And no one knows what the meat-eater Baryonyx did with its great sharp claws. Its long jaws and teeth show that it probably fed on fish, the way crocodiles do. Did it catch big ones with its curved hooklike claws? That is the only idea scientists have had so far.

Iguanodon, its cousins, and many hunters were part of a long procession of dinosaurs. Different kinds lived at different times. After one kind died out, another appeared. Then it, too, died out. Most of the long-necked plant-eaters were gone by the time Baryonyx began to do its fishing. And Baryonyx had disappeared when a new and fierce giant hunted the next group of plant- eaters.   39

40

King of the Tyrants

Tyrannosaurus is the most famous of all the terrible hunters. It was the largest and scariest member of the meat-eating tyrannosaur family, and that is how it got its name, which means "tyrant dinosaur."

Like you, all dinosaurs have two names. Usually we just call them by their first names, but there was one tyrannosaur that was so big and so fierce that we sometimes like to add its second name, "rex," which means king. Tyrannosaurus rex was the king of the tyrants, the most powerful of them all.

Tyrannosaurus could take huge bites with its enormous teeth. It could have swallowed a young plant-eater whole.

But could Tyrannosaurus run fast enough to catch any creature that was quick on its feet? Some people used to think that Tyrannosaurus could only waddle along slowly. Perhaps, they said, it depended for most of its food on animals that had already died.

Other scientists disagree. They have studied the tyrant's legs and knees, and they are quite sure that Tyrannosaurus could have raced along at 40 miles an hour.

Bone Heads

Tyrannosaurus had eye sockets that faced forward. It could see better than most other meat-eaters because it could look straight ahead with both eyes at the same time. That helped to make it the king of hunters.

The bones of Tyrannosaurus' snout and forehead were very thick. Why? Scientists think that Tyrannosaurus may have used its head the way mountain sheep use theirs today. When two big male sheep want the same mate, they have a butting contest. They bang their heads together, and when one gets tired and quits, the other is the winner.

Another great head-banger that lived at the same time was plant-eating Pachycephalosaurus. The bone on the top of its head was nine inches thick, and a contest between two of these giants must have sounded like gunfire. The bones where the head joined the neck were specially formed so the two animals didn't knock themselves out.

Micropachycephalosaurus

But were those thick domes used only for mating contests? Perhaps they had another use, too. Perhaps Pachycephalosaurus wasn't afraid to back off and ram into a tyrannosaur that was threatening to eat it.

Pachycephalosaurus had a tiny cousin with a big name—Micropachycephalosaurus. It was so small that Tyrannosaurus could have squashed it flat beneath one heavy toe.

Pachycephalosaurus

More and Different Hunters

At the time when tyrannosaurs roamed Earth, other giants often hunted nearby. As in earlier times, not all these meat-eaters were dinosaurs. Winged Quetzalcoatlus, soaring on the lookout for a meal, made a shadow like that of a small airplane. Elasmosaurus, with its very long neck, ate fish in the sea. Phobosuchus, a monster crocodile, could catch a young dinosaur if one came too near the swamp where it lived.

Perhaps the great crocodile could even have rushed at a grown-up dinosaur called Struthiomimus and grabbed it by one of its long hind legs. Struthiomimus and its cousins are called ostrich dinosaurs because they were built much the way ostriches are today. Struthiomimus had a sharp beak but no teeth. Possibly it ate anything it could catch, including small birds. Or perhaps it lived on insects. Scientists aren't sure.

An even greater mystery is the dinosaur called Deinocheirus, which means "terrible hand." The huge sharp claws on its fingers tell you why it got its name. Its arms were 12 feet long, but they may not have been as scary as they look. They resemble the much smaller arms of the ostrich dinosaurs. So the terrible hands may just have caught lizards or other small creatures. And that is all we can say about Deinocheirus, because scientists have never found bones from the rest of its body.

Phobosuchus

44

Deinocheirus bones

Quetzalcoatlus

Elasmosaurus

Struthiomimus

Warning: Don't Bite

Only a very hungry meat-eater would have tried to take a bite out of Ankylosaurus or any of its cousins in the ankylosaur family. Knobs and plates of bone covered their heads and backs. Extra protection came from the sharp spikes arranged on various parts of their bodies.

One ankylosaur, Edmontonia, was as heavy as a pickup truck, and its shoulder spikes pointed forward. If meat-eaters came too close, it could charge at them, stab them in their legs, and knock them over.

With the dainty little scalloped teeth in its square jaws, how did Edmontonia get enough to eat? Maybe it ate a lot of berries. Or perhaps it nipped off tough leaves and gulped them down whole. Then its stomach could have churned and crushed the leaves with stones it had swallowed. Polished belly stones that might have helped digest rough food were found with one Edmontonia skeleton.

Ankylosaurus

Euplocephalus

Edmontonia

Ankylosaurus and Euplocephalus had some special defenses of their own. In addition to the heavy bones on their heads, they had bony eyelids that could snap shut to protect their eyes. And their long tails ended in huge balls of bone. Powerful muscles in their tails and hips would swing the ball so hard that it could break a meat-eater's shins.

47

Duckbills Large and Small

The ankylosaurs had neighbors called hadrosaurs. The first ones ever found had snouts that looked rather like duckbills, so scientists gave them that nickname. People thought that duckbills, like ducks, must have spent their time wading and swimming in lakes, eating water plants.

Then scientists began to study the duckbills' amazing teeth. Some had as many as two thousand teeth arranged in many rows with sharp tips sticking out like the edge of a bread knife. Two thousand teeth, if lined up in a single row, would stretch out across a basketball court!

With teeth like those, a duckbill didn't need to live on mushy food. It could chew and grind and mash and soften twigs or leaves from tough land plants—even pine needles and berry bushes.

At first, no one knew much about duckbill babies. Then a scientist discovered a nest full of duckbill eggs. He went on exploring and found many more nests nearby. This had been a place where great numbers of dinosaur mothers laid their eggs and took care of their babies. One nest held the fossil skeletons of some young dinosaurs. Perhaps a tyrannosaur had attacked the mother, and the babies had starved to death in the nest.

48

Duckbill Crests and Calls

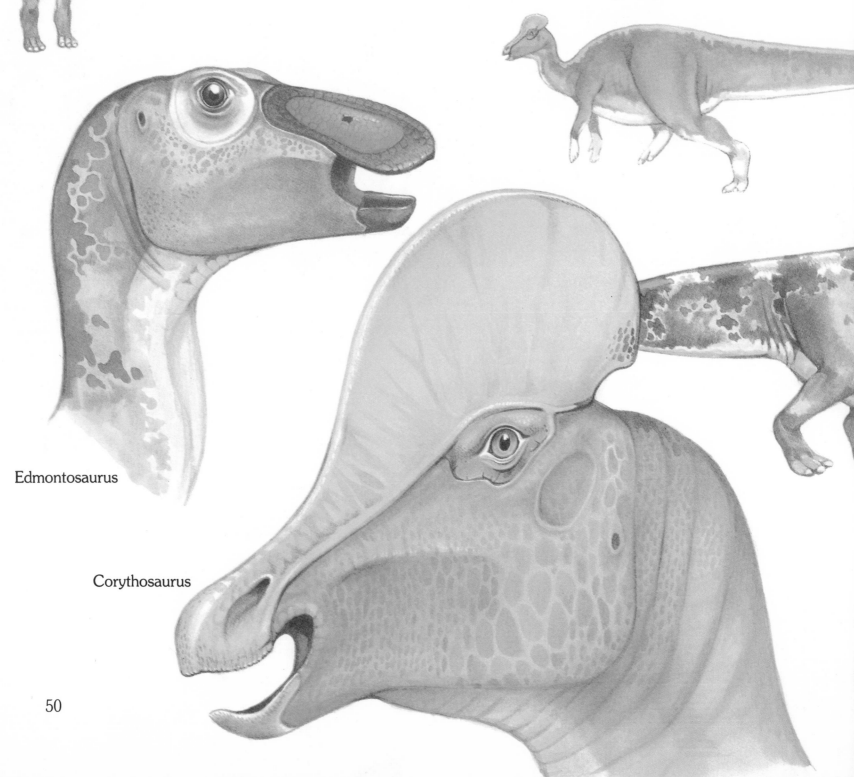

Enormous herds of duckbills once lived on the wide plains between rivers and mountains. There were about 30 different kinds, some very large and others quite small. Each kind had its own special head shape. About half had skulls that were rather flat, with or without a low bony ridge or crest on top. The others had tall and hollow crests.

What could have been the use of these tall, strange-shaped bones? Scientists know that duckbills often traveled together. Perhaps the crests helped the members of each group to find each other when several

Edmontosaurus

Corythosaurus

50

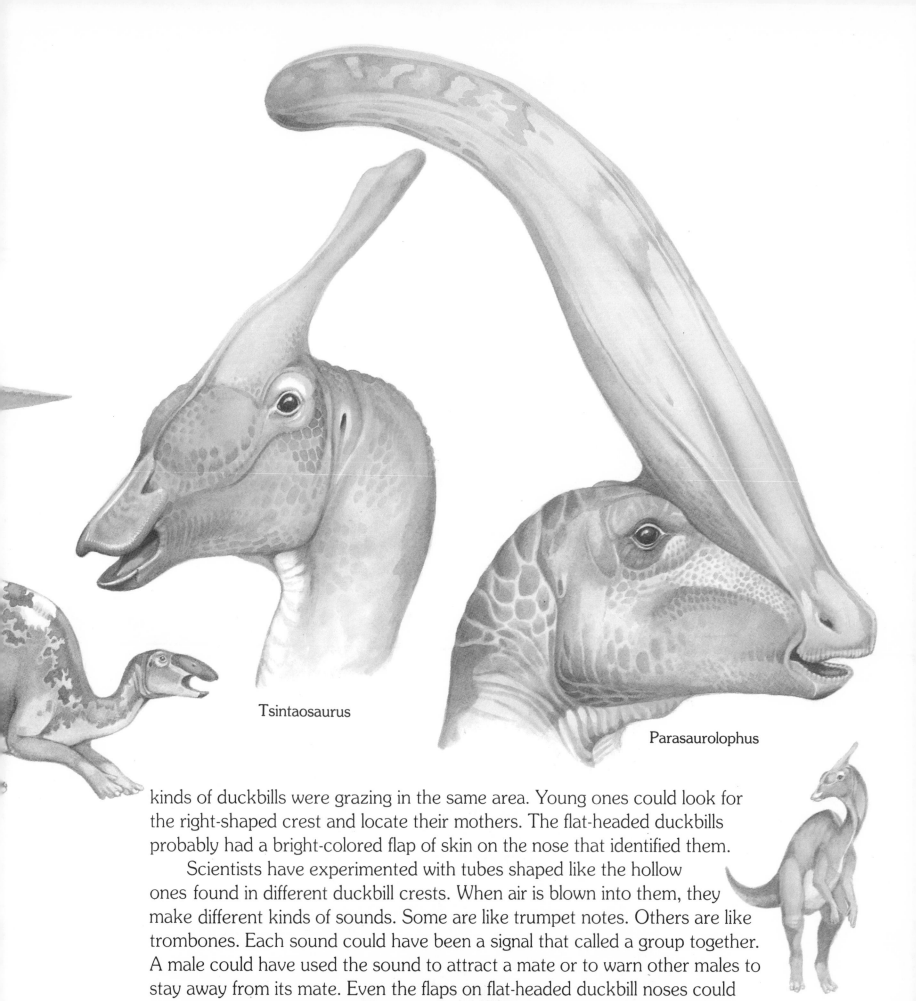

Tsintaosaurus

Parasaurolophus

kinds of duckbills were grazing in the same area. Young ones could look for the right-shaped crest and locate their mothers. The flat-headed duckbills probably had a bright-colored flap of skin on the nose that identified them.

Scientists have experimented with tubes shaped like the hollow ones found in different duckbill crests. When air is blown into them, they make different kinds of sounds. Some are like trumpet notes. Others are like trombones. Each sound could have been a signal that called a group together. A male could have used the sound to attract a mate or to warn other males to stay away from its mate. Even the flaps on flat-headed duckbill noses could have been used for snorting. Duckbill country must have been a noisy place where everyone could snort, toot, bray, bugle, trumpet, whiffle, or moo. 51

The Last of the Giants

Remember little Styracosaurus and its narrow escape from the giant meat-eater? The styracosaurs belonged to a family of dinosaurs called ceratopsians, which had horns on their heads. Their long, heavy skulls ended in sheets of bone called frills that stuck up at the back of their heads.

The bony frill probably helped to protect against a meat-eater's bite, but scientists think it had other uses, too. Gigantic muscles connected the frill to the lower jaws. With one strong pull, the jaws could snap shut and bite off the toughest tree branch.

More than a dozen kinds of frilled dinosaurs strutted about or traveled together in large groups in search of food. Like duckbill crests, their frills may

also have served as signals to other members of each group. To young ones, the message was, "You are not lost—here we are." Male ceratopsians could show off their frills to attract females. Or one male could be signaling to another, "I dare you to wrestle. I am the boss!"

Torosaurus and Triceratops were the mightiest ceratopsians. From the top of the frill to the tip of the beak, each of their heads was eight or nine feet long. Each of these giants weighed as much as an elephant. But in spite of their size, they were quick on their toes, and with their great sharp horns they were probably a match for any meat-eater—even Tyrannosaurus rex.

Triceratops

Tyrannosaurus rex

54

What Happened to the Dinosaurs?

Why are none of these strange and wonderful dinosaurs alive today? Fossil collectors have thought up more than two dozen possible answers to that question, and scientists are still discussing it. They know that about 65 million years ago the last of the dinosaurs died. So did many other animals. Some scientists think that a comet or an asteroid struck Earth and created an enormous dust cloud that shut out sunlight. Without the sun, lots of plants died. Plant-eating dinosaurs and many other animals had no food, and they died, too. Meat-eating creatures died soon afterward. Other scientists think perhaps the weather changed too much in other ways for dinosaurs to stay alive. Or diseases could have killed them. One scientist even thinks all these theories may be right.

The long dinosaur story has not ended. Most scientists agree that long ago Archaeopteryx, or some small dinosaur, was the ancestor of our birds. Remember that the next time you hear a robin singing after a rainstorm.

After the Dinosaurs

What was the world like after the last dinosaur died? Most places became rather quiet. Crocodiles still bellowed in swamps, but the rumble of great dinosaur herds was gone. Insects still chirped and buzzed. Frogs croaked. Birds called. Several kinds of small furry creatures squeaked and squealed and chattered. They were the warm-blooded animals called mammals.

At first the mammals were too small to make much noise, but after a while new and larger ones began to appear. Then some of them died out, and different ones developed. This happened again and again.

At first many mammals resembled the ones we know. There were ratlike creatures, and there was one animal that looked a bit like a squirrel. But then came a whole procession of strange big mammals. Some were as weird and as fascinating as any dinosaur. For a while gigantic meat-eating birds fed on smaller creatures. Later, large meat-eating mammals took their place.

Of course, not all the ancient mammals developed into huge creatures. The ancestors of our rabbits, chipmunks, cats, dogs, and other small animals were also living and changing, alongside the ancestors of elephants and giraffes.

One especially important group of mammals was the primates—our own ancestors. Fossil bones, very much like our bones, have been found in rocks that are more than three million years old. But scientists are not sure just when true human beings first appeared. Perhaps we will never know exactly when people began to talk and sing and wonder about things. It must have happened when brains grew bigger and developed a complicated top part— the part sometimes called the "thinking cap."

Dinosaurs never developed very big brains, but the brains they had were good enough so that they got along very well in their world. Thanks to your thinking cap, you can get along in our complicated world and even learn to spell Micropachycephalosaurus.

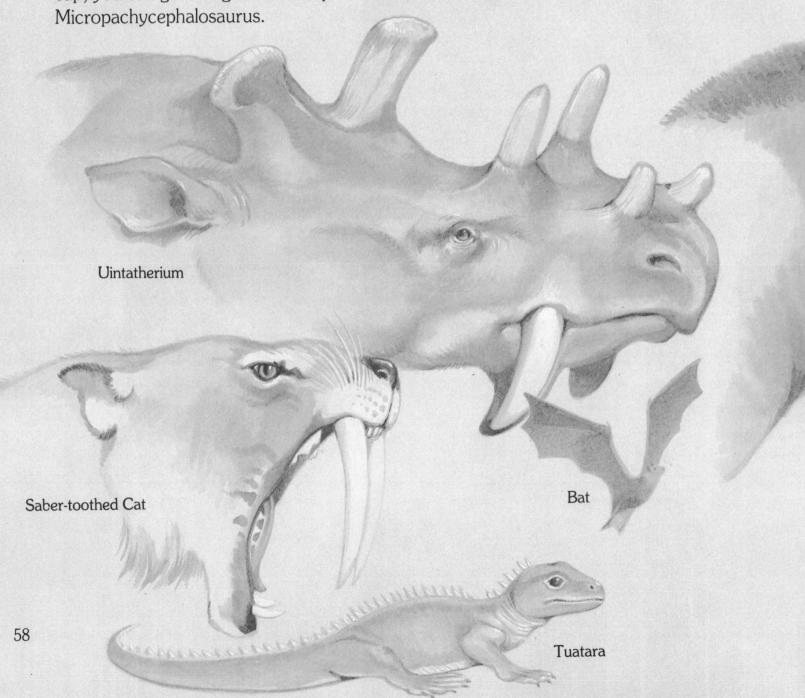

Uintatherium

Saber-toothed Cat

Bat

Tuatara

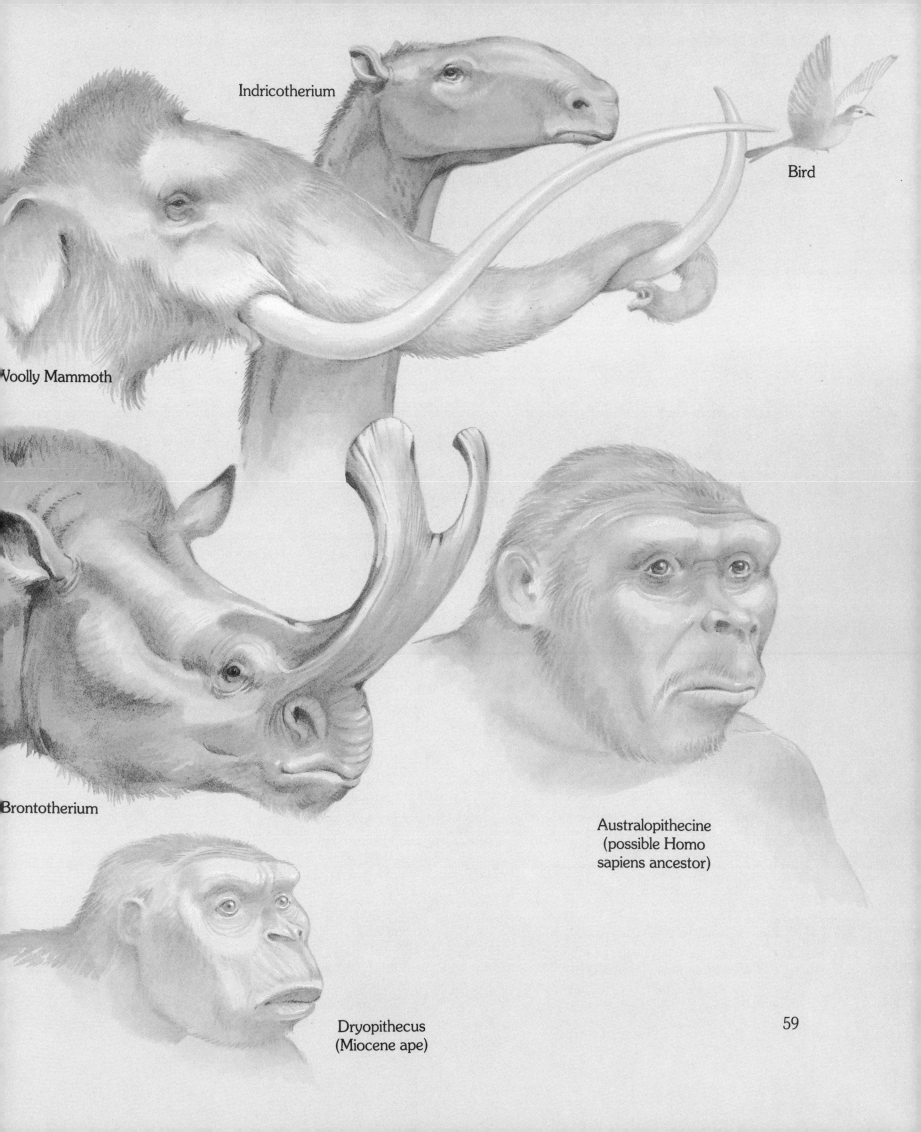

Indricotherium

Bird

Woolly Mammoth

Brontotherium

Australopithecine
(possible Homo
sapiens ancestor)

Dryopithecus
(Miocene ape)

Index